SLEEPOVER AT GRAMMA'S HOUSE

Barbara Joosse

illustrated by **Jan Jutte**

Philomel Books • An Imprint of Penguin Group (USA) Inc.

For Lucia Anabel, my "little light."   —*Granna*

For Patti Gauch, editor, mentor and friend.   —*J.J.*

Goodie goodie goodie . . .

I'm packing up my little trunk
my little overnighty trunk

my nighty in my nighty trunk.

Goodbye little fish and little fish
flakes
and everything in the regular
place.

Goodbye my mom
goodbye my dad

goodbye you
baby in the bed.

Well I'm going there this minute
to the Gramma who is in it
and the Doozie who is barking
and I'm bouncing bouncing bouncing
and I'm flipping off my shoesies
and I'm rolling down my socksies
and I'm sighing
and I'm singing

and I'm . . .

THERE!

Oh.

We love each other so.

Gramma silly
silly millie silly millie
"Let's put paper over the doorway
so we can run through!"

Ta-DA!

We put on pinky party hats
one for Gramma
one for Doozie one for me
then we set the table fancy
with a razzle and a dazzle
and a horn to hootie tootie
to make the party start.
TOOOT!

Oh.

We love each other so.

Gramma silly
silly millie silly millie
"Now I know what we can do—
you paint me and I'll paint you!"
And then . . .

Oh.

We love each other so.

Tick tock tick tock it's time
for the sleep-tight nighty-night ball
all righty righty righty
in my little pink nighty
night ball.

Oh-dee-doh.

Dancing on my gramma's toes.

"I want a story! I want a story!"
Gramma says in her little kid voice.

Oh how my honey loves to play
"you be the gramma and I'll be the little kid."

"Once upon a time" I say in my gramma voice
"there was a very BIG child and a teeny tiny gramma.

The child never ever sat on Gramma's lap because then she would squash her flat.

The End."

"YAAAY!" Gramma says.
"I want another story.
I want another story."

Oh, I love my honey so
of course I say
"OKAY!"

Once upon a time there was a cake that nobody ate.

nd then they did.

The End."

Tick tock tick tock tick

rrrruuuuumble!

At the tippy-end of our sleepover day
we like to finish up this way . . .

snuggled and together
on the pitter patter porch
on the ricky rocky swing.
"Ooooooh!" watch the lightning
sky writing.
"Ahhhhh!" hear the thunder
rain rumbling.

This we know—
the very best way to fall asleep
is inside a hug.

Oh.

We love each other so.

Patricia Lee Gauch, Editor

PHILOMEL BOOKS
A division of Penguin Young Readers Group.
Published by The Penguin Group.
Penguin Group (USA) Inc., 375 Hudson Street, New York, NY 10014, U.S.A.
Penguin Group (Canada), 90 Eglinton Avenue East, Suite 700, Toronto, Ontario M4P 2Y3, Canada (a division of Pearson Penguin Canada Inc.).
Penguin Books Ltd, 80 Strand, London WC2R 0RL, England.
Penguin Ireland, 25 St. Stephen's Green, Dublin 2, Ireland (a division of Penguin Books Ltd).
Penguin Group (Australia), 250 Camberwell Road, Camberwell, Victoria 3124, Australia (a division of Pearson Australia Group Pty Ltd).
Penguin Books India Pvt Ltd, 11 Community Centre, Panchsheel Park, New Delhi - 110 017, India.
Penguin Group (NZ), 67 Apollo Drive, Rosedale, North Shore 0632, New Zealand (a division of Pearson New Zealand Ltd).
Penguin Books (South Africa) (Pty) Ltd, 24 Sturdee Avenue, Rosebank, Johannesburg 2196, South Africa.
Penguin Books Ltd, Registered Offices: 80 Strand, London WC2R 0RL, England.

Design by Semadar Megged.   Text set in 18.5-point Triplex Serif.
The illustrations were created in ink, watercolor and acrylic.
Printed at RR Donnelley
Reynosa, Tamaulipas, Mexico
April 2010
ISBN 978-0-399-25261-7